Salt-Water Moon

Salt-Water Moon

David French

Talonbooks • Vancouver • 1988

published with assistance from the Canada Council

Talonbooks
201 / 1019 East Cordova
Vancouver
British Columbia   V6A 1M8
Canada

Typeset in Baskerville by Pièce de Résistance Ltée.; printed
and bound in Canada by Hignell Printing Ltd.

First printing: March 1988

Salt-Water Moon was first published by Playwrights Union of
Canada, Toronto, Ontario.

Canadian Cataloguing in Publication Data

French, David, 1939-
  Salt-water moon

  A play.
  ISBN 0-88922-257-6

  I. Title.
PS8561.R45S3 1988   C812'.54   C88-091164-6
PR9199.3.F74S3 1988

Once again,
For my parents

Salt-Water Moon was first produced at the Tarragon Theatre, Toronto, in October, 1984 with the following cast:

JACOB MERCER   Richard Clarkin
MARY SNOW   Denise Naples

Directed by Bill Glassco
Set & Costumes by Sue LePage
Lighting by Jeffrey Dallas

Salt-Water Moon transferred to the Bayview Playhouse in November, 1984, with the original cast.

THE CHARACTERS

Mary Snow
Jacob Mercer

THE PLACE

The front porch and yard of the Dawes' summer house in Coley's Point, Newfoundland.

THE TIME

An August night in 1926.

The front porch of a house that was built in the last half of the nineteenth century, probably by a ship's captain or local merchant. It has a solid feel about it, this porch. You just know that the interior of the house would consist of oak banisters and newel posts, wide halls and high ceilings. And that every timber was hand-chosen and pit-sawn and constructed by men who built houses the way they built boats—to last.

On stage right of the porch is a rocker.

There is not much of a yard, because they built their houses close to the sea in those days to make easy access to the waters where they made their living. In fact, the house stands quite close to a road that runs in front of it, a gravel road skirting the rocky embankment that holds back the sea. Some indication of this road should be on the set, though it need not be realistic.

It is a lovely night in August, 1926. A warm night in this tiny outport at the edge of the sea, a night lit by the full moon and a sky full of stars.

At rise: MARY SNOW is alone on stage. She sits on the front step, training a telescope on the sky. MARY is seventeen, a slender, fine-boned, lovely girl with short black hair. She is wearing a short-sleeved yellow satin dress and black flat-heeled shoes. She wears no makeup except for a slight hint of red on her cheeks. The only jewellery she wears is her engagement ring.

Slight pause. Then MARY rises and crosses into the stage left part of the yard and again peers at the sky through the telescope.

A moment later JACOB MERCER's voice is heard offstage, singing faintly as though he were some distance down the road stage right. His voice carries so faintly, in fact, that MARY spins around and faces that direction, listening intently, not sure whether it is her imagination.

JACOB: *to the tune of "Pretty Redwing"*
  'Oh, the moon shines bright on Charlie Chaplin,
  His boots are crackin' for the want of blackin',
  And his baggy trousers they want mendin'
  Before they send him, to the Dardanelles.'

MARY stands riveted to the spot, her eyes searching the shadow-pocketed road, almost afraid of what might walk into view, but still straining to listen . . . . But the song has ended, and there is only silence. With an inward shrug, she assumes it is imagination—the ghost of last summer—and resumes her study of the stars.

At that moment JACOB MERCER appears on the road stage right. He is about six months older than MARY, a solidly-built, good-looking young man in a store-bought suit and brown fedora. In his right hand he holds a cardboard suitcase held together with a rope tied in a half-hitch knot. At first sight of MARY, he instinctively sets down the suitcase and removes his hat. He watches her so intently it is as though he is holding his breath . . . . Finally, JACOB clears his throat, and MARY whirls around, startled. They stand motionless, staring at one another for a long moment.

JACOB: *finally*
  Hello, Mary. *then* Aren't you even going to acknowledge me? *Pause.* The least you could do is make a fist.

MARY: *Beat. Quietly*
It *was* you I heard . . .

JACOB:
What? Just now?

MARY:
I heard your voice on the road, and I said to myself,
No, it couldn't be him . . .

JACOB:
It is.   *then*   Why? Who'd you t'ink it was, a
spirit? The ghost of Bob Foote roaming the roads?
Poor Uncle Bob in blackface out for a last howl at the
moon?

MARY:
That's not funny, Jacob.

JACOB:
It wasn't meant to be.

MARY:
Making fun of the poor old soul, and him tonight in a
closed casket. It's not right.

    Slight pause.

JACOB: *crosses slowly to the porch*
Don't tell me you still believes in spirits? I can hardly
credit it, a young girl like you.   *He nods at the
house.*   The Right Honourable and Lady Emma
must find it some odd.   *He sets down the suitcase.*

MARY:
I don't see what's so odd about that, believing in
spirits.

JACOB:
Don't you?

11

MARY:

No.

JACOB:

What? Looking at the sky t'rough a spyglass and over
your shoulder for ghostes? *pronounced 'ghostus'*
You don't find that odd?

MARY:

No. Neither do Mr. and Mrs. Dawe.

JACOB:

Then Jerome must, him being a schoolteacher. He must
wonder who in the world he's become engaged to.

MARY:

Just because I takes an interest in the stars, Jacob,
don't mean I shuts my eyes to the wonder that's
around me. Now do it?

JACOB:

I suppose not.

MARY:

The day Father died in the Great War, Mother saw
him at the foot of the bed in Hickman's Harbour. He
was killed at Beaumont Hamel, more than two
t'ousand miles away, yet mother woke up to find him
standing side-on to the bed, and she stared at him, she
said, till he faded into the light of morning.

JACOB:

I knows. I've heard you tell it.

MARY:

Well then. *She turns away.*

Pause.

JACOB:

Oh, look, Mary, it's a shame to get off on the wrong foot after all this time. I'm sorry I said that. It just slipped out.

MARY:

What?

JACOB:

That crack about old Bob looking like a bootblack. I never meant to make light. That's just me.

MARY:

No odds. I don't imagine Mr. Foote minds now.

Slight pause.

JACOB:

It's bad enough that he's dead at all, but to come home looking like the ace of spades . . . Must be tough on Mrs. Foote.

MARY:

No mistake.

JACOB:

I saw the wreath on the door as I was passing, so I went inside to pay my respects. There was a crowd in the parlour, the closed casket sitting on two wooden chairs. I figured it was Mrs. Foote inside, till she walked out of the kitchen with the Right Honourable and Lady Emma. Figured old Bob was still on the Labrador along with Father and wouldn't be back till next month.

Slight pause.

MARY:

He was sitting in the bunkhouse, they said, and bent down to take off his boots. He died before he hit the floor.

Slight pause.

JACOB:

Is it true what I heard? Is it true Mrs. Foote went down to the wharf yesterday to meet the mailboat? Hoping to get a letter from Bob?

MARY:

True.

JACOB:

Instead there's a pine box on the deck with his body in it. And Bob in that box all packed in salt.

MARY:

It's a sin.

JACOB:

Takes t'ree weeks for the boat to get here. And him burnt black from that rock salt. Jesus.

Pause.

Still, he couldn't have picked a nicer night for a wake, could he? It's some lovely.

Pause.

It's that bright out I bet I can read the hands on my pocket watch.   *He removes his watch from his vest pocket.*   Look at that. Ten to ten. I can pick out the maker's name, almost: Tisdall . . .   *winding the stem for something to do*   . . . Yes, maid, it's some night. Not the best time to be studying the stars, though. Not with a full moon.   *Slight pause.*   It's hard to see the stars with the naked eye on a night like this. I suppose that's why you'm using the spyglass.   *Slight pause.*   What kind is it?

MARY:
Yes, you can't wait to hear the answer, can you?
Standing there with your eyes afire, drooling to hear
what make of telescope.

JACOB:
Don't be foolish.

MARY:
Well, as if you cares what make it is, Jacob Mercer.
You're just spitting out the first words that pop in your
mouth.

JACOB:
I wouldn't have to, Mary, if I wasn't made to feel a
stranger.

MARY:
Well, you *are* a stranger.

JACOB:
I wasn't once.

MARY:
You are now.

JACOB:
Suit yourself.

    Pause.

    almost to himself   Some welcome home this is.

MARY:
What did you expect, a band? A band with me at the
head, clapping my hands: 'Why, it's the Prodigal Son,
boys! All the way back from Toronto! Strike up the
drum!'

JACOB:
Now who's making fun?

15

MARY:

You're lucky I'm still speaking to you! Some wouldn't let you step foot in the yard!   *She sits on the step.*

Pause.

JACOB:

All I asked just now was a simple question. There's no call to be sarcastic.

MARY:

Isn't there?

JACOB:

No. It don't become you. A yellow dress becomes you, Mary, more than sarcasm . . . Not that you don't have every right to be cross. I don't blame you, I suppose.

MARY:

So you shouldn't.

JACOB:

No. You have every right to carry a grudge. Every right in the world. I'm the first to admit it. Besides . . .

MARY:

Besides what?

JACOB:

Besides, I already knows the make of spyglass. It's called a Black Beauty. We have one at the house. Father got it from a Sears-Roebuck catalogue back in 1902. Ours has a cracked lens.

MARY:

Oh, you t'ink you're some smart, don't you? Well you're not, Jacob Mercer. And you're not one bit funny, either.

JACOB:
> That's not what you used to say.

MARY:
> I'm learning all about the stars now. That's more than
> I ever learned with you. I can see the satellites of
> Jupiter with this telescope, and the mountains of the
> moon.

JACOB:
> Imagine that. Imagine that cold white eye up there
> with mountains in it.

MARY:
> The moon has more than mountains. The moon has
> valleys and seas and bays. All as dry as a biscuit,
> Jerome says. All with beautiful names.

JACOB:
> Such as?

MARY:
> Ocean of Storms, for one. Sea of Rains. Bay of
> Rainbows. Lakes of Dreams.

JACOB:
> That's the only water Jerome McKenzie could sail
> without getting his socks wet, the Lake of Dreams.

MARY:
> Don't you start in on Jerome, either. He knows a lot
> more than you gives him credit for.

JACOB:
> A year ago you wouldn't have said that. A year ago
> you had your own notions about the moon. Remember
> that?

MARY:
> No.

JACOB:

You don't recall saying the Man in the Moon was set there for not obeying the Sabbath? He wasn't good enough for Heaven, you said, so God set him betwixt Heaven and Earth. You don't recall saying that?

MARY:

No.

JACOB:

Sure you do. I had a toothache that night, and we walked to Clarke's Beach so's Billy Parsons could charm my tooth. 'Don't pay him,' Mother said. 'Mind now. And don't t'ank him, either, or the charm won't work.' Oh, that was some night.

MARY:

I don't recall.

JACOB:

You don't seem to recall very much, suddenly, and you with a memory on you like a camera.

MARY: *rises*

Well, perhaps it suits me not to remember. As if you're any different. You remembers only what you wants to remember, Jacob, and the rest you forgets.   *She starts up the steps.*

JACOB:

Like what?

MARY:

Like what?   *turns to face him*   Like running off last August, that's what! Or has that suddenly slipped your mind?

JACOB says nothing.

Didn't have the courage to say goodbye, did you? Not so much as a card in the past year!

JACOB:
> I'm no good with cards . . .

MARY:
> You wrote your mother.

JACOB:
> Once.

MARY:
> Twice.

JACOB:
> Twice then.

MARY:
> I saw her at church that Sunday just before we went back to St. John's in the fall. She told me you was boarding with Sam and Lucy Boone on Oakwood Avenue. Working for the Fairbanks Block and Supplies.

JACOB:
> Yes. Making concrete blocks.

MARY:
> A whole year you've been gone, boy, and now you just walks in off the road. Steps off the nine o'clock train in Bay Roberts and expects me to recall some old night when Billy Parsons charmed your tooth. Are you forgetting I'm spoken for?

JACOB:
> I'm not forgetting.

MARY:
> Then you haven't changed one bit, have you? Still the same, in spite of your fancy hat! Still the schemer!

> *Pause.*

JACOB:

It wasn't just some old night, and you knows it. A lot happened that night besides my toothache.

MARY:

A lot's happened since.

JACOB:

I suppose.

MARY:

Too much.

JACOB:

Perhaps.

MARY:

Then don't keep dragging up what's best forgotten. Leave it buried.

JACOB:

Can't be done, Mary. Nights like this brings it all back . . . The smell of honeysuckle on the road. The new moon that night like a smile over the Birch Hills. A smile that became a grin. Remember that?

MARY:

Yes, a lot you noticed the moon.

JACOB:

Indeed I did.

MARY:

You hardly gave it a second glance. Stumbling along the road to Clarke's Beach, your hand tight to your jaw. Whimpering like an old woman.

JACOB:

I don't recall.

MARY:

No, you wouldn't.

JACOB:

You wasn't much comfort, if it comes to that. Harping on spruce gum every inch of the way.

MARY:

I mentioned it once.

JACOB:

Once?

MARY:

Once. 'Why don't we get some spruce gum?' I said. 'That'd kill the pain.'

JACOB:

And where in the name of Christ would we find a black spruce in the dark of night? That's like telling a drowning man to head for shore.

MARY:

Oh, go on with you.

JACOB:

Spruce gum. My Jesus.

MARY:

Lucky for you we made it to Clarke's Beach. 'Shoot me, Mary! Put me out of my anguish!'

JACOB:

I never said that, now.

MARY:

Then strutting in to Billy's like you was dropping in for tea. White with pain but still with a grin. Snapping your braces with the same hand you'd just been gripping your jaw with all the way from Coley's Point.   *pronounced Cōley's*

JACOB:

> I don't want to argue with you, Mary. I never come all this way to fight.

MARY:

> 'Oh, by the way, Billy. I almost forgot to mention. I have a pain in my tooth.'

JACOB:

> Drop it, I said.

MARY:

> It's all coming back now.

JACOB:

> He put his finger on my tooth, Billy did, and prayed, and seconds later the pain left. That's it.

MARY:

> 'Sorry to trouble you, Billy. Next time I'll just get spruce gum.'

JACOB:

> Once you gets going, you can't stop, can you? No mistake.

MARY:

> I'll never forget the walk home, either. How often you stopped to admire the sky. How often you stopped to tie your laces.

JACOB:

> It worked, didn't it?

MARY:

> Yes, it worked. By the time we got back the Dawes had locked me out. Just as you planned.

JACOB:

> We spent the night up on Jenny's Hill, the two of us. And the rest, as the preacher said, is history.

MARY:

　　Yes.　　*Beat.*　　Ancient history.

　　Slight pause.

Besides, the Dawes don't lock me out now: I'm older.
I'm seventeen now and more responsible.

JACOB:

And just as superstitious, in spite of Jerome. Old Bob
Foote was the same. He wouldn't go in the woods
without a scrap of bread tied up in a red hanky to
ward off the fairies. Christmas Eve he was too scared
to go nigh the barn. Claimed the horses got down on
their knees to pray.

MARY:

Scoff all you wants to, boy. I'd like to see you walk
past the graveyard alone on a dark night, without
whistling.

JACOB:

Oh, don't be foolish. There's not'ing to be frightened
of. Unless it's one of the boys up to his mischief. Like
the time Bob Foote got the scare of his life, the poor
soul.

MARY:

Why? What happened?

JACOB:

Didn't you hear? He was walking past the Church of
England this night, old Bob was, and one of the
boys—I t'ink it was Wiff Roach—was got up in a red
sheet and a pair of cow horns. And just as Bob got
abreast of the graveyard, out pops Wiff from behind a
tombstone.

MARY:

Oh, my God.

JACOB:

That's not the best part. Old Bob is whistling along past the church, walking on the balls of his feet, like someone trying to tiptoe t'rough life, a finbone of a haddock in his vest pocket . . . when all of a sudden he sees this big shadow 'cause Wiff has his back to the moon. The shadow drops down over Bob Foote like the wings of the Angel of Death, and he gives a shriek and spins around. And there's Wiff with his arms out wide and he growls at old Bob, 'Bob Foote,' he says, 'I'm the Devil, my son, and I've come to get you!'

MARY:

Oh, what a sin.

JACOB:

And Bob sings out at the top of his voice—   *He drops to his knees and clutches his hands in a gesture of entreaty.*   —'Don't harm me, Devil, for the love of Christ! I'm married to your *sister!*'

> *MARY laughs, in spite of herself. JACOB laughs along with her.*

MARY: *finally*

Oh, you. You almost had me believing. Well, you just wait. Some dark night you'll be walking home alone and it won't be Wiff Roach you hears behind you. I wouldn't make fun, if I was you.

JACOB:

Go on with you.

MARY:

Just you wait.

JACOB:

That's all old foolishness.

MARY:

It is, is it?

JACOB:
   Old wives' tales.

MARY:
   What if I told you I saw a Jackie Lantern this
   summer? What would you say to that?

JACOB:
   Now, Mary.

MARY:
   I did.

JACOB:
   A Jackie Lantern? One of those lights that's supposed
   to come after dark and carry off bad little girls and
   boys?

MARY:
   My mother saw it, too. The both of us.

JACOB:
   What? You've been to see her?

MARY:
   Just after we arrived here this summer. Mrs. Dawe let
   me go home for a week. I took the train to Clarenville
   and the boat to Random Island. All by myself.

JACOB:
   I don't suppose she recognized you?

MARY:
   I didn't expect her to. I was only nine years old the
   last time I saw her. That still bothers her, I can tell,
   that she had to put Dot in a Home and me into
   service. But what could she do? When Father was
   killed, she'd slip into those queer moods that still
   haven't left her. Moods that last for weeks on end,
   staring at the floor, forgetting to comb her hair . . .

25

Anyway, I went to Hickman's Harbour like I said, and we was sitting out on the porch one night, when along comes this ball of light. It floated up from the shore and bobbed straight for the churchyard.

JACOB:
A ball of light?

MARY:
Yes. I've never seen the like of it. It was as bright as any star in the sky tonight.

JACOB:
Was it blue?

MARY:
Yes . . .

JACOB:
That figures. I saw a light like that once. My first and last summer on the Labrador. The Skipper called it St. Elmo's fire.

MARY:
Are you making this up?

JACOB: *hand on heart*
The God's truth.

MARY:
All right then.

JACOB:
I was ten years old. Father was still fighting in France, so I was the head of the family. I marched down to Will McKenzie's store and signed on. Jerome was helping out. He gave me my crop: my oilskins and rubber boots, and salt beef and sugar for Mother. I made twenty-four dollars for six months, and that was fishing from sunrise to starlight, and out of that come twelve dollars for the cost of my crop. I never went at it again, I can tell you.

MARY:
What about the blue light, Jacob?

JACOB:
I'm getting to it . . . . The men have a custom, Mary,
if it's your first time across the Strait of Belle Isle. One
of the men gets all dolled up like Neptune. Up he
climbs over the bowsprit, the God of the Sea, with a
razor in his hand and a bucket of tar.

MARY:
What's that for? The razor and tar?

JACOB:
That was *my* first question.

MARY:
Was there an answer?

JACOB:
I soon found out. They held me down on the deck, the
men did, whilst Neptune shaved off all my hair and
tarred my face.

MARY:
Now that's one sight I would've paid to see. You must
have looked some fright.

JACOB:
Blacker than Mr. Foote looks now in the last night of
his wake . . . I sat apart on the deck that night, away
from the other men. Too ashamed to be seen . . .
That's when I saw your light, Mary. It was perched
atop the mizzenmast. A ball of light, just pulsing away.

MARY: *relishing the comparison, almost tasting it on her tongue*
Like a blue star.

JACOB: *Beat.*
Like a what? . . .

MARY:

You heard me. Like a blue star.

JACOB:

Go on with you. Stars aren't blue.

MARY:

Some are. Some are blue, some are red, some are yellow. There's a blue star in the sky this very minute. The fourth brightest star in the summer sky.

JACOB:

Is that a fact?

MARY:

Indeed it is. I've seen it myself. It's in the Constellation of the Harp.

JACOB:

The Constellation of the Harp?

MARY:

Yes, the Constellation of the Harp. So there.

JACOB:

Show it to me then.

MARY:

No, you're just making fun of me. Besides, I've wasted enough of my time. I've got t'ings to do.

JACOB:

Like what?

MARY:

Like what?

JACOB:

Yes, like what?

MARY:

Lots of t'ings.

JACOB:
Name one.

MARY:
Well, like . . . like that suit of Mr. Dawe's. He wants
it pressed for the funeral tomorrow. He's one of the
pallbearers.

JACOB:
Yes, I suppose that wouldn't look right, would it, for
the Right Honourable Henry Dawe, Member of
Parliament, to look less than his best? Not with the
Orange band leading the hearse and all hands in back
stepping to the beat of the Death March. No, that
wouldn't look right. Him in his black crepe armband
and white gloves and a suit he might've slept in.

MARY:
That's right.

JACOB: *Beat. Smiles.*
Look, why don't you just show me the blue star and
then I'll be on my way? It'll only take a minute.

MARY:
Will you promise to go, if I shows it to you?

JACOB:
I promise. Word of honour.

MARY:
All right then, I'll show you the blue star. But only
because you don't believe me. I wants to see you choke
on your own smirk . . . .   *She walks away and turns
to face him.*   First off, you have to know where the
Big Dipper's at.

JACOB:
The Big Dipper? Sure, any fool knows where that's to.

MARY:
 Where?

JACOB: *points*
 Right there. Right over Spaniard's Bay. And up above it's the Little Dipper pouring into it.

MARY:
 Come here then, and I'll show you the blue star . . .

 JACOB gets behind her, close.

MARY:
 Now pay attention. I'll tell it the way Jerome does, so you'll always find it yourself in future. You watching?

JACOB:
 Oh, I'm all eyes, Mary.　　*He breathes in the fragrance of her hair as though bending before a bouquet of wildflowers.* All eyes, ears, and nose.

MARY: *disturbed by his closeness*
 All right, now. First off . . . First off, keep your eye on the Big Dipper. That's where we starts from. Now you see those . . . those . . . ?

JACOB:
 Those what?

MARY: *takes a step away*
 Those two stars that makes up the left side of the bowl? Those two?

JACOB: *edging closer*
 Which two?

MARY: *impatiently*
 Those two! . . .　　*Although she remains facing away, she is acutely aware of his closeness.*　　Now pretend your finger is a pencil. What you does is you runs a line between those two stars, like this, and you . . .　　*She swallows hard.*

30

JACOB:

 You what?

MARY:

 You keeps on going and runs the line straight up like
 this, up and up and up . . .

JACOB:

 Up and up and up . . .

MARY:

 Yes, until you're at the Constellation of the Harp.
 That's those six stars right there. See? One, two, t'ree,
 four, five, six . . .

JACOB:

 Don't look much like a harp to me.

MARY:

 No odds. That's its name. The Constellation of Lyra.
 L-y-r-a. That means harp in a dead language.

JACOB: *Beat.*

 What's that you sprinkled on yourself tonight? Smells
 as nice as fresh bread. What is it, vanilla?

MARY: *turns on him*

 All right, that's it for you, boy! That's it!

JACOB:

 What? . . .

MARY:

 I'm not wasting my time a second longer! Remain
 ignorant all your life! See if I cares!

JACOB:

 I was paying attention, sure.

MARY:

 Indeed you wasn't!

JACOB:
Indeed I was.

MARY:
What did I do then? Show me.

JACOB:
All right, I will.

MARY:
And just the way I told it, mind.

JACOB:
Word for word . . . You took your finger like a stick of pencil and you drawed a line betwixt those two stars there, and you kept on a line as straight as a plumb up to the crown of the sky, till you struck the Constellation of Lyra, which means harp in Greek.

MARY:
Latin.

JACOB: *his finger raised straight overhead*
All right, Mary, what now? I can't stand here all night, reading the sky like Braille. What's next?

MARY:
That's it, boy. That's Vega you're pointing at.

JACOB:
Vega?

MARY:
The blue star! Look!   *She thrusts the telescope at him.*   See for yourself!

> *JACOB takes the telescope and aims it at the star. While he has the telescope to his eye, MARY studies him secretly.*

JACOB:

Well, I'll be . . . ! It is so blue. Look at that. Almost as blue as St. Elmo's fire . . . *He turns to MARY—slyly.* Where did you say the red star was?

MARY:

Never you mind where the red star's to. Next it'll be the yellow one. Find it with your naked eye, I'm going inside.

MARY reaches for the telescope but JACOB backs away.

Give me that!

JACOB:

No. Not till you shows me a red and yellow star.

MARY:

The yellow one's the sun! See it in the morning! Now give me the telescope!

JACOB:

Anger don't become you, Mary, any more than sarcasm. Makes your knuckles white and scrunches up your face.

MARY:

You promised, Jacob!

JACOB:

I promised I'd go; I never said when.

MARY: *Beat.*

All right, there's a red star in the Little Dipper, if it's that important to you. Hurry up and look.

With deliberate slowness JACOB trains the telescope on the sky.

JACOB:

So there is, Mary. A red star in the corner of the bowl . . . Like the Devil had one eye and was staring down at me. Winking.

MARY:

No mistake.

JACOB:

The way he prob'bly winked that night on Jenny's Hill, though neither one of us noticed. Did you ever tell Jerome about that night?

MARY:

He knows all there is to know.

JACOB:

All?

MARY:

Yes, I told him everyt'ing.

JACOB:

That you didn't.

MARY:

Not that there was much to tell.

JACOB:

That's more like it.

MARY:

Well, there wasn't.

JACOB:

Keep saying that, Mary, you might convince yourself. I doubt it would take much to persuade him otherwise. All his life long, Jerome, he'll be scratching his head and pondering: 'Did she? Or didn't she?'

MARY:

Listen, I wants you out of this yard, and right away. I don't want you here when Jerome gets back. Is that understood?

JACOB:

Now that's odd. First you tells me you have to get in soon and put on the flat-iron for that black serge suit of the Right Honourable's. Then the truth slips out, don't it? Just as smooth as the lie you told.

MARY:

It's none of your business, one way or the other. I don't have to answer to you now. So go on!

JACOB:

I wondered why you had on your good dress tonight, with a touch of red on your cheeks. What's that from? Still using the red paper inside the lid of a Cocoa tin?

MARY:

What odds if I am?

JACOB:

All dolled up for Jerome McKenzie, is that it? You and the moon just waiting for the Cock of the Rock to pull up in his Touring car?

MARY:

That's right. What of it?

JACOB:

What'll you do then, the two of you? Sit here a spell and gaze at the sky?

MARY:

We might.

JACOB: *imitating JEROME, an earnest and studious young man*
'The distance betwixt the earth and moon, Mary, is . . . oh, let's see . . . one hundred t'ousand miles, give or take an eighth of an inch.'

MARY:

It's a quarter of a million miles, stupid, and he don't
speak like you.

JACOB:

My God, Jerome has some fund of useless knowledge,
don't he? Teaches Grade Eleven in that t'ree-room
schoolhouse, but give him a fishknife, he'd slit his own
t'roat.

MARY:

Why should he be cleaning fish? He's a schoolteacher,
and a good one. He knows a lot more than you'll ever
know.

JACOB:

Is that a fact?

MARY:

Yes, it's a fact.

JACOB:

Well, ask him what happened on the morning of July 1,
1916 and see how much he knows.

MARY:

Any schoolchild in Newfoundland knows what
happened on July 1, 1916.

JACOB:

Oh, no doubt he could tell you the entire
Newfoundland Regiment was wiped out at the village
of Beaumont Hamel in the first battle of the Somme.
Out of seven hundred and fifty men, only forty not
dead or wounded. That he might know. But could he
tell you what the weather was like that Saturday
morning? How the sun rose on a lovely summer day,
with a mist on the valley floor, and poppies in scarlet
patches, and clouds making shadows that raced over
the green fields of Picardy? Could he tell you that?

How one regiment after another was wiped out—the Royal Dublin Fusiliers, the Border Regiment, the Essex. And then it came the Newfoundlanders' turn. Colonel Hadow walked twenty yards forward and gave the signal. The Captain blowed the whistle, and the men went over the top, heading straight into the German cross-fire, knowing they was walking alone t'rough the long grass of No Man's Land into certain death. Not a single man flinched or looked back, just kept on walking in perfect drill formation, the sun glinting off their bayonets. Could he tell you what all the observers noticed that day as the Newfoundland Regiment walked into the storm of machine-gun bullets and mortar shells: how all the soldiers to a man tucked their chins into their forward shoulders like sailors leaning into a gale of wind? Could he tell you that? . . .

>   *MARY says nothing.*

. . . No, and that he couldn't. 'Cause his own father wasn't there to tell him the real story, was he?

MARY:
All the men couldn't enlist, could they?

JACOB:
My father volunteered, didn't he, goddammit? And so did yours. Only yours is buried today under the bronze statue of a caribou in the fields of France.

MARY:
Father enlisted for the same reason yours did. Will McKenzie wasn't in that position.

JACOB:
No, he didn't need the dollar a day they paid. The same wage as the Canadian privates. More money than he'd ever made in his life, Father. More money than he could make at fishing, especially when he went into collar to a merchant like Will McKenzie. That's a term

I bet Jerome never explained to you, in collar. He's prob'bly too busy pulling on his oars in the Lake of Dreams to explain the real world.

MARY:

I knows what it means, in collar.

JACOB:

What?

MARY:

It means to sign aboard a fishing schooner. The fishermen go into collar the first of May and come out of collar the end of October when the schooner is moored for the winter.

JACOB:

Yes. 'The first of May is Collar Day/ When you're shipped you must obey.'

MARY:

If your father had been a shareman, Jacob, he would've come out of collar as soon as the voyage was over last summer, as soon as he tidied up his traps. No odds if they did come home early.

JACOB:

But he wasn't a shareman, was he? He only shipped out for wages. Which meant that Will McKenzie had him in collar for another two months and could do what he liked with him!

MARY: *Beat.*

All right, but what you're feeling right now, Jacob, had only to do with that, what Will McKenzie did to your father last summer. There's no need to take it out on his son.

JACOB:

Even Mrs. McKenzie did more for the war effort than her husband. At least she knitted socks for the Women's Patriotic Association.

MARY:

Most of the women did, sure.

JACOB:

Yes, and all Will McKenzie could do was wait for a
brave man to march home so's he could whittle him
down to size seven years later. The same man who was
part of the famous Blue Puttees, same as your own
father. The same man who crawled t'rough the
trenches at Gallipoli in 1915 in his tropical fit-out,
twenty-seven days on the firing line without taking off
a stitch or having a wash. The same man who endured
the November storm they called the worst in forty
years, with two hundred men swept away in the
flooded trenches or frozen to death when the rains
stopped and the killing frost set in. Rubbing their feet
with whale oil and stuffing 'em into sandbags filled
with straw . . . He'd sit in the mud at Suvla Plain
and try to eat a piece of bread and jam, and the flies
that t'ick the bread would be black before he could get
it to his mouth—the same flies that bred in the corpses
in No Man's Land . . .

MARY winces, and turns away.

. . . He still wakes up in a sweat, Mother says. Rats are
crawling over him, the way they done in the trenches
in France. Rats bigger than cats snapping at his boots
and stepping over his face in the dark, their whiskers
tickling his ears . . . But the worst of the dreams always
start the same way: with the women in black ploughing
the fields, no more than the fling of a stone from that
tiny French village, July 1, 1916. The day he faced the
German guns and lived, lying wounded in No Man's Land,
with that tin triangle of the 29th Division on his back
—a piece of metal cut from a biscuit tin and painted
red. He couldn't move an inch or the tin would glint
in the sun and the snipers would pick him off. So he
lay there under that blazing sun of July till dark came,
pressing his pain into the bloodied earth beneath him.
One of the men the Germans called the 'White Savages.'

And this is the same man, Mary, that was under the t'umb of Jerome's father last summer and had to do what he was told, the law being the law, Military Medal or no!   *He has to turn away to hide the rage that makes him want to smash the moon from the sky.*

Pause.

MARY:

Look, you can't keep picking away at that, Jacob, or the wound will never heal . . .

JACOB:

I don't expect it to. All I asks, Mary, is that you don't stand there and defend him to my face. The fact that you'm marrying his son next month is bad enough.

MARY:

I can't help who Jerome's father is, can I? Any more than he can. Any more than I can help who mine was.

JACOB:

Go on with you. Jim Snow was a brave man. The one the stretcher bearers found closest to the German wire that night when they went out to collect the dead.

MARY:

Yes, and a lot of good it done, his courage. He left behind two daughters and a wife who can't look after us. Ten years later she still sets his plate at the table. Still keeps his boots polished. She sits in the rocker now with a look on her face as though she's forgotten somet'ing . . . Some days she walks out in the road and looks down it, the way she did that day when he left to catch the boat for Clarenville and the train to St. John's. She saw him turn the bend in the road, she said, and he was gone. Vanished from her life like a stranger . . . I've often wondered why she let him go at all. I'd never let a husband of mine go off to war, I guarantee. I would've marched into that camp at Pleasantville and dragged him out by the scruff of the neck.

JACOB:

> I wouldn't worry too much about Jerome. With his
> eyesight, he'd never get past the medical exam . . .
> By the way, where's he to? Standing in front of the
> looking-glass in Country Road, polishing his bald spot?

MARY:

> No, he is not standing in front of the looking-glass. He
> drove Doctor Babcock to French's Cove. Betty
> Tucker's in labour.

JACOB:

> He could be quite a spell then, couldn't he? Last time
> Betty had twins . . . That would serve him good and
> right, wouldn't it? Leaving you here alone, with a
> moon in the sky and an old sweetheart fresh off the
> train?

MARY:

> Yes, one I can't wait to get rid of.

JACOB:

> No. One who'd sooner look at a yellow satin dress with
> you inside it than the blue star of Vega. One with no
> bald patch on the crown of his head, and him only
> twenty years old.

MARY:

> He can't help that, can he? That runs in the family.

JACOB:

> You ever watch him on the sly, Jerome? How he yanks
> out the hairs one by one and bites 'em?

MARY:

> He does no such t'ing. Besides . . .

JACOB:

> What? Besides what?

MARY:

Besides, Jerome says bald-headed men are more potent. So there.

JACOB:

Potent? What's potent?

MARY: *Beat.*

Well, I didn't ask him at first. I was afraid he'd t'ink I was ignorant . . .

JACOB:

It prob'bly means dull as a turnip and twice as t'ick.

MARY:

It don't mean that at all. I looked it up in that dictionary Mr. Dawe keeps on a stand in the parlour. It means . . . strong.

JACOB:

Strong? Yes, I'd like to see Jerome McKenzie go into battle with sixty-six pounds of gear: his haversack, his gas helmet and goggles, a rolled-up ground-sheet . . .

MARY: *cutting in*

It don't mean strong like that, potent. It means . . .

JACOB:

It means what?

MARY:

Well, it's more like . . .

JACOB:

Like what? Spit it out.

MARY:

Well, like . . . like in the *Book of Genesis.*

JACOB:

The *Book of Genesis?*

MARY:

    Yes. Do you recall how Lot and his two daughters
went up in the mountains after God destroyed Sodom
and Gomorrah? And how the daughters hatched a plan
to get their father drunk and sleep with him?

JACOB:

    I'm not likely to forget that story. They told us in
Sunday school to skip it.

MARY:

    That first night in the cave, remember, the older
daughter lay with Lot, and the second night they got
him drunk again, and the younger one crawled in.

JACOB:

    I remembers. So?

MARY:

    So the older one had a son and she called him Moab;
the younger one had a son called Ben-ammi.

JACOB:

    Look what's all this to do with Jerome? Has he been
crawling in with his mother?

MARY:

    Oh, don't be foolish . . . So according to the Bible,
Lot gave each of his daughters a child, and not only a
child but a son, and him after bedding down with each
only that one time apiece.

JACOB:

    Imagine.

MARY:

    And not only that, boy, but he was half-asleep, the
poor old soul, and so drunk he didn't know what he
was up to. I t'ink that's what they means by potent.

JACOB:

So Jerome told you he was potent, did he, like Lot in the *Book of Genesis*? Oh, that's a good one, that is.

MARY:

That's not what he said, and you knows it. I was just explaining what the word meant.

JACOB:

I suppose he couldn't wait to tell you that, could he? That must've preyed on his mind all last summer. Slinking around here, his cloth cap on his head, his shoes all shined.

MARY:

Why shouldn't he drop in? Mrs. Dawe and his mother are sisters.

JACOB:

Yes, and him with a bag of oranges or peppermint candies, and neither of the Dawes with a sweet tooth. Oh, he didn't fool me for a minute.

MARY:

Stop it, Jacob. I don't want to hear any more. I means it.

JACOB:

Looking sheepishly t'rough those spectacles like he had a secret too large to bear. Well, tonight, Mary, the cat is out of the bag. The secret is loose in Coley's Point at last: JEROME MCKENZIE IS POTENT!

MARY:

Oh, hush up, boy! You want him to hear you in French's Cove?

JACOB:

What odds? He'll just suppose the word is out and puff up his chest like a blowfish. Next he'll be drawing a stallion on the blackboard and asking his class, 'Guess who?'

MARY:
I'm not listening to this a second longer! I'm going inside! Goodbye! . . .   *as she starts up the stairs*   And don't walk off with that telescope, either, or Mr. Dawe will have your head!

JACOB: *bitterly*
What cradle will you be using, Mary, once your first child comes? Jerome's old one? That hardwood cradle his father bought him as a child?

> *This stops MARY just as she opens the screen door. She hesitates, standing with her back to JACOB.*

It has a lovely antique finish, don't it? Last a lifetime, that cradle. You can set it on the porch on a nice day and rock your first child. Sing him a song to the creak of your foot on the rocker . . .

> *MARY slams the door, turns and gives JACOB a reproachful, almost defiant look that makes him turn away.*

. . . Sing him a sea chanty all about the good ship, *Trinity*, in the summer of '25. How she sailed out of Bay Roberts harbour in the spring of the year bound for the Labrador and how they struck an east wind and put into Harbour Grace to wait it out. How Captain Abe Wheeler hired a driver to take him back to Bay Roberts, and when he come back two weeks later, the wind was just shifting. All the men, Father included, was in their bunks when the Captain stepped aboard, but he couldn't say a word to the others: they was sharemen. Father was lying there with his boots out over the bedboard, when he heard Captain Abe say, 'So this is what you do behind my back, eh, Esau?' 'I wasn't doing no harm behind your back,' says Father. 'We woke up this morning and the day was fair. We done all the work we could.' They went up on deck and had more words. Father was not the sort to take dirt from any man. 'Go below,' says Captain Abe,

'and get in the bunk!' 'And that I wunt,' says Father.
'Go below, I said, and get in the bunk!' says Captain
Abe. 'No,' says Father, 'I wunt.' The Captain looked
over at old Bob Foote. 'Bob,' he says, 'go fetch the
constable.' Old Bob lowered his eyes and didn't move.
'Do as I say, Bob,' he says. 'Take the punt and fetch
the constable.' Still Bob wouldn't move . . . At last
Father said, 'No odds, Bob, I'll go below.' And he
went down and got in his bunk and stayed there till
Captain Abe told him to get up. It was either obey or
be clapped in jail for six months! . . .

MARY: *gently*
You mustn't do this to yourself, Jacob. It's going to eat
you up alive . . .

JACOB:
What? A lovely sea chanty that every child in
Newfoundland should learn by heart? How the *Trinity*
came back early that year with a poor catch, and how
the merchant looked around for someone to take it out
on and his eyes settled on Esau Mercer, the only one
who wasn't a shareman, the only one who had crossed
the Captain that trip. He marched Father up to his
house in Country Road, Will McKenzie did, and
brought out the hardwood cradle that belonged to
Jerome as a child. He sat Father down in the chair on
the porch and told him to rock the cradle, and that's
what Father done, day in, day out, from morning till
dark, his foot going up and down, up and down on the
rocker of that empty cradle, till he was out of collar
two months later . . .   *He stands in the yard, his face
raised, still trembling from the memory of his father's shame.*

    Slight pause.

MARY:
That cradle, Jacob, will never be rocked by *my* foot,
rest assured of that.

JACOB:
No?

46

MARY:

No. I won't allow it in my home, and Jerome knows it.

JACOB: *Beat.*

You'll be having your own home, will you? You must want it some bad.

MARY:

Yes, and in a month's time I'll have it. No more carrying the breakfast tray to someone else's bedroom. Shining someone else's silver. Polishing another's floor like a looking-glass. I've been in service since I went with that old Mrs. Jessup in St. John's. The one who locked me in the closet for taking a piece of butter. Well, once I steps in my own home, I won't be locked up or locked out. I won't be browbeaten or chastised, or ordered here, ordered there. And any breakfast tray I carries will be for my own husband or children, and any silver I shines will be from my own service, and any floor that I can see my face in will show only *my* face looking up and no one else's chin over my shoulder. My children will not be taken from school before the year's out and sent to the Labrador so's they never can get an education. They'll go to Bishop's Feild College in St. John's, the same as Jerome, and they won't go near the sea, not even to get their socks wet, not even in the lake of Dreams! So goodbye!
She exits into the house and slams the door.

Slight pause.

JACOB: *to himself*

By the Christ, Jacob, that's some wonderful girl . . .   *He removes his coat and sets it on the railing. Smoothing down his hair, he walks to the door and knocks.*   Mary!   *then*   Mary Snow from Hickman's Harbour! Come out, Mary, and look at the moon! There's never been a night like this before, and there'll never be another!   *then, taking a new tack*   Say, Mary, did you hear about the time the

47

King paid a visit to St. John's? They decided to introduce him to the oldest person in Newfoundland, which was Miss Snook from Heart's Delight. In honour of the occasion, the King was to present Miss Snook with one hundred and four brand new dollar bills, one for each year of her life. When it was over, the King took Miss Snook aside. 'Miss Snook,' he said, 'it must be wonderful to be one hundred and four years old and in such good health. Tell me,' said the King, 'was you ever bedridden?' 'Only twice, me baby (*rhymes with 'abbey'*),' said Miss Snook. 'Once in a haystack out behind the barn and once in an old dory.' *He listens. Then he walks down the steps into the yard and faces the house.* Come on out, Mary. Don't be like that. Sometimes I gets carried away, that's all. I'm no different from you in that respect . . . You'm prob'bly peeking t'rough the curtains right this very minute, wondering to yourself, What's that fool up to now? Where do he get the gall to be standing in the yard of the Right Honourable Henry Dawe, Member of Parliament, waking up the half of Coley's Point that isn't at the wake? . . . And won't Lady Emma be some cross, once she finds out the girl she's had in service for four years is causing a disturbance loud enough to start old Bob Foote knocking on his casket? . . . *peers in the window* And poor Jerome, let's not forget him. He might be persuaded to call off the wedding, once he discovers that Mary Snow was carrying on with an old flame . . . *walks farther into the yard* So you decide for yourself, Mary, 'cause I'm not budging. I'll just make myself at home, till Jerome comes driving down the road, innocent as the day he was born. Won't it give him a lesson in life, to find a wolf in the yard and the lamb cowering behind the curtains? . . . *He crosses quickly to the porch and sits in the rocker. Begins to sing "Wedding in Renews."*
'There's going to be a jolly time,
I'll have you all to know,
There's me and Joe and Uncle Snow
Invited for to go.

I have the list here in my fist,
So I'll read out the crews,
There's going to be a happy time
At the wedding in Renews.

louder   There's Julia Farn, from Joe Batt's Arm,
She's coming in a hack;
And Betsy Doyle from old Cape Broyle,
She'll wear her Sunday sack;
And Prudence White, she's out of sight,
She'll wear her dancing-shoes.
We'll dance all night till the broad daylight
At the wedding in Renews.'

The door bursts open, and MARY comes striding out.

MARY:
    Will you stop that! My God, what's wrong with you? I
    never would've said hello in the first place had I
    knowed you'd carry on like this! Now go home!

JACOB: *rises from the rocker*
    Suit yourself, maid. It's just that I t'ought you might
    like to see what I brought you all the way from
    Toronto. It's in my suitcase.

MARY:
    I don't want it, whatever it is. Just go.

JACOB: *crosses down the steps to the suitcase*
    Is that what they teaches you in the Church of
    England? To slap the gift from a man's hand before
    you've even seen it?   *He sets the suitcase on the ground
    and undoes the rope.*   Now close your eyes.

MARY:
    No . . .

JACOB:
    Turn away your head then, or it won't be no surprise.

MARY:
Oh, for . . .   *Exasperated, she crosses down into the yard
and stands with her back to JACOB.*

*JACOB opens the suitcase and brings out a pair of silk
stockings. He removes them from the package and drapes
them delicately over his outstretched arm.*

JACOB:
Now you can look.

MARY does. Slight pause.

Well?

*MARY says nothing. She takes an involuntary step and
stops. From the look on her face you'd be hard-pressed to
know whether she liked the stockings, except for one thing:
she can't keep her eyes off them. She stands several yards
from JACOB, staring almost quizzically at his
outstretched arm.*

You can touch 'em, maid. They won't burn you . . .

MARY remains at her distance, unmoving.

. . . Feel how smooth the texture is. Pure silk . . . A
dollar a pair at the Timothy Eaton store on Queen Street.
I bought a pair for you and a pair for your sister. You
can give 'em to her the next time you'm in St. John's.

MARY: *still not moving*
They don't allow her to wear t'ings like that. The
Matron is strict.

JACOB:
What? Not even a pair of good stockings?

MARY:
No. I took her one of my dresses one time and they
wouldn't allow her to have it.

50

JACOB:
Why not?

MARY:
'Cause all the girls at the Home have the same uniform: black button-up shoes, navy blue kneesocks, a short navy blue skirt with pleats, a navy blue cardigan, and over that a cotton pinafore with flowers on it.

JACOB: *Beat.*
Well, take both pairs for yourself then. Would you?

MARY:
I can't be accepting gifts from you now, Jacob. It's not right.

JACOB:
Well, I can't be taking them home, can I? Mother would crack me across the skull if I walked in the door with these on my arm.

MARY:
Yes, and what would Jerome say if he heard I'd taken those? Has that crossed your mind?

JACOB:
Jerome? The hell with him. If he can bring you oranges last year, I can bring you stockings now.

MARY:
That was different.

JACOB:
What's different about it?

MARY:
I wasn't spoken for last year, that's what's different.

JACOB:

> We was keeping company, wasn't we? That's almost
> the same. Did that stop him from slouching in that
> rocker there, darting a look at you every time he
> sucked his pipe?

MARY:

> You make it sound as if we couldn't get rid of him. He
> may have dropped in once a week, if that.

JACOB:

> Once was enough. For all the notice he took of me, I
> might've been one of his students he stuck in a corner
> and forgot. *mockingly* Tapping his Briar pipe in
> the pit of his hand. Pointing the stem at the sky.
> 'Look, Mary, there's the evening star, now. Venus.'

MARY:

> What odds? I was no more taken with Jerome last
> summer than the Man in the Moon. What's happened
> since is your own fault and no one else's.

JACOB:

> Sure. Rub salt in the wound.

MARY:

> It's true, isn't it?

JACOB:

> For Christ's sake, Mary, I was seventeen at the time.
> Seventeen!

MARY:

> That's no excuse! You was old enough to lure me up
> to Jenny's Hill, wasn't you? And two months older
> when you kept me waiting for the sound of your boots
> on the road, and me still here when Mr. Dawe was
> ready to blow out the lamp!

JACOB:

> That was wrong, I admit.

MARY:

> The next day I walked down to your house. 'Oh, he left,' your mother said. 'Sure, didn't he tell you? Took the train to Port aux Basques this morning. You must've just missed him.'

JACOB:

> She had it wrong. I didn't go straight to Port aux Basques. I got off in St. John's. I worked unloading the steamers, till I had enough for my passage and Travelling Certificate . . .

MARY:

> I walked up the road that morning, and every step of the way I could feel your mother's eyes on my back. I went straight to Mrs. Dawe. 'I wants to go up to Toronto, Mrs. Dawe,' I said. 'There's somet'ing I have to do there.' 'What?' she said. 'I can't tell you,' I said, 'but it's important.' 'Well, I'm sorry, Mary, but you can't go. You still owes us twenty-four dollars for that bridge you had put in.' 'I won't go for good,' I said. 'Just for a week or two.' 'No,' she said, 'it's out of the question.'

JACOB:

> What was it you had to do, Mary? Why just a week or two?

MARY:

> It would've taken me that long to hunt you down. Then I would've put on my prettiest dress and knocked on your door. And when you stuck your head out, I would've slapped your face so hard it would've knocked you into the next room. But at least I'd have had the satisfaction of saying goodbye.

JACOB:

> I'm sorry. I wanted to tell you goodbye. I tried to, two nights before I left here . . .

MARY:
Two nights before? Yes, I noticed how hard you tried two nights before. The way you sat on the step and looked at your fingers. The way you shuffled off home without a backward glance.

JACOB:
The words wouldn't come . . .

MARY:
That must've been a first, mustn't it?

JACOB:
Perhaps.

MARY:
You'd been so upset the past week. Ever since your father came home from the Labrador. Always working late at Taylor's tinsmith shop.

JACOB:
I couldn't go home till he was fast asleep. I didn't want him to have to see me . . .

MARY:
It never occurred to me I was the one on your mind that night. All along I supposed it was him, your father.

JACOB:
It was the both of you.

MARY:
No mistake.

JACOB:
It was. There was a moment there when the boat pulled out of Port aux Basques for North Sydney, for Canada, when I almost jumped over the side.

MARY: *pained*
Why didn't you?

JACOB:

    I can't swim.

MARY:

    That's not funny, Jacob.

JACOB:

    I wasn't *being* funny . . . I stood on the stern of the
    Caribou, looking back at land for the longest
    time . . . It was a grand day, too, the sun shining, the
    breeze making t'umbprints on the blue water. It almost
    felt good to be alive . . .

MARY:

    I suppose you never gave a second t'ought to me, did you?

JACOB:

    Indeed I did.

MARY:

    Out of sight, out of mind.

JACOB:

    It wasn't like that at all. It's just that . . .

MARY:

    What?

JACOB:

    It's just that I couldn't forget my father's face. The
    look on his face that day as he raised his head on Will
    McKenzie's porch and caught me passing. I never
    wanted a son of mine to see such shame in his father's
    eyes. Nor a wife of mine to have to look on me with
    such pity. The way my mother looked, later on, as we
    all sat down to supper, him with his eyes on his plate,
    hardly able to swallow a mouthful . . . The broken
    look on those two faces made me turn and walk to the
    bow of the boat that was pointed for another
    country . . .

JACOB pauses, and without looking at MARY, walks to the suitcase. He folds in the stockings. Closes the suitcase and ties the rope. All the time MARY watches him.

MARY: *finally*
So I didn't count, is that it? What was I, Jacob? Just the girl you frolicked with one night on the cliffs of home?

JACOB:
That's not true, now.

MARY:
Don't say it's not true, it *is* true. The simple truth is your father mattered more. It was what you saw on that summer porch, wasn't it, that drove you away from here?

JACOB:
Well, it's no whim that's carried me back, I guarantee.

MARY:
I never believed it was.

JACOB:
And don't suppose I haven't tried to forget you since, because I have. I tried to shut you out as best I could, but . . .

MARY:
But what?

JACOB:
Somehow you'd always . . . always creep back in . . . Then I heard about you and Jerome . . .

MARY:
Who told you?

JACOB:
Mother wrote. For a minute I figured she'd become feeble-minded. 'Not Jerome McKenzie,' I said to Sam Boone. 'She must mean another Jerome.'

MARY:

What if it had been someone else? Would that have made any odds? *then* Would it?

JACOB:

No. Not a bit.

MARY:

I wonder . . .

JACOB:

I sat on my bed that day and read the letter, and when I come to the part about you and Jerome, the words made my ears ring. I had to go to the window for air . . . It was like . . .

MARY:

Like what?

JACOB:

Almost like . . . like I'd swallowed a hook lodged so deep inside it was there for good. For the first time I felt what a fish must feel, with a foot on his head and his guts being ripped out . . . I quit my job. I tramped the streets from the crack of dawn. Up one street, and down the other, till my soles wore out. I got in a fight with a fellow on Yonge Street. He come at me with an ice-pick. I put my hands behind my back and I said, 'Go on, buddy, put it right there!' I said. *He smacks his heart.* 'Come on!' I said. 'Do it! I won't make a move to stop you!' . . . He backed off and looked at me like I'd just escaped from a strait-jacket. Dropped the ice-pick and took off up the street . . . I went back to Sam Boone's that night and packed my bag. I said to his wife, 'Lucy,' I said, ' I t'ink it's time I went home . . .'

Slight pause.

MARY:
Well, you ought to have saved yourself the trip. What you ought to have done, Jacob, is had your shoes cobbled and took to the streets again. Till you walked me out of your system.

JACOB:
Once was enough. All I got was blisters.

MARY:
What did you expect I'd do, boy? Cancel the wedding next month? Hurt someone the way you hurt me? Did you imagine I was pining away that much? My God, you must t'ink a lot of yourself, don't you? All you have to do is walk across the Klondike into Coley's Point, and I'm expected to feel the same? Expected to feel grateful?

Slight pause.

JACOB:
Do you love him?

MARY:
What odds to you? He's a good man, Jerome. He's quiet and kind, he's smart and dependable, and once he builds his own house in Country Road, we're taking Dot to live with us.

JACOB:
That's not what I asked, Mary. He may be all of those t'ings you said, and more. I don't give a damn if he's wise like Solomon or strong like Samson. I don't care if he builds ten houses in Country Road for you and your sister. I only asked if you loved him.

MARY:
Why wouldn't I love him? I'm marrying him, aren't I? *She turns away.*

JACOB:
That still don't answer my question. Look at me, Mary . . .

MARY:
What for? . . .

JACOB:
Look me in the eye and tell me you loves him, and I'll walk out of this yard and never come back.

MARY:
You made one promise tonight you never kept. You can't be trusted.

JACOB:
Try me once more. Tell me you loves Jerome McKenzie, and you'll never see the dust of my feet again.

MARY:
All right, and I'm holding you to it. *She turns and stares straight at him.*

Slight pause.

JACOB:
You can't say it, can you? *then* Can you?

MARY:
I loves him. There. I said it.

JACOB: *Beat.*
No odds. I don't believe you. *He walks away.*

MARY:
No, you wouldn't believe the Devil if he snuck up behind and jabbed you with his fork.

JACOB:
That I wouldn't.

MARY:
No. All you believes is what you wants to believe.

JACOB:

No, I believes in what's real. I believes in a young girl trembling at my breath on her neck. That's what I believes in.

MARY:

What young girl?

JACOB:

There's only one in the yard that I can see.

MARY:

And just when was I trembling?

JACOB:

When? I'll tell you when. When you pointed out the blue star of Vega tonight, and I stood behind you. I could feel you shaking under your dress like a young bride at the altar.

MARY:

It's chilly out!

JACOB:

Indeed it's not chilly out, or where's your shawl to? . . . Your heart was pounding, wasn't it? *then* Wasn't it?

MARY:

Next you'll be telling me you could hear it.

JACOB:

No, but I could see the pulse in your neck, Mary, beating like a tom-tom.

MARY:

The Bible's got it all wrong. It's not the women who are the vain ones, it's the men.

Slight pause.

JACOB:

You ought to wear yellow more often, maid. It really do become you. Suits your black hair and fair complexion.

MARY:

Is that what you did the past year up in Toronto? Sweet talk the girls?

JACOB:

What girls?

MARY:

'What girls?' he says.

JACOB:

There wasn't any girls, sure.

MARY:

No, and autumn don't follow summer, I suppose?

JACOB: *Beat.*

All right, perhaps there was one or two girls . . .

MARY:

One or two? Is *that* all?

JACOB:

T'ree or four at most.

MARY:

You don't need to exaggerate. And you calls Jerome a blowhard for boasting of somet'ing he never claimed to be in the first place?

JACOB:

He claimed to be potent, didn't he?

MARY:

That's all he claimed to be, not'ing more. And he said it as a joke, more or less.

JACOB:
> More or less?

MARY:
> I'm sorry I ever told you, now.

JACOB:
> He's in the wrong place, Jerome is. He ought to try
> Toronto. The girls up there haven't set eyes on a
> decent man since the day I left.

MARY:
> Yes, and I suppose all four was waving you off at the
> station? Running down the tracks? Blowing you kisses?
> 'Don't forget us, now! Come back soon!'

JACOB:
> No. Only the two.

MARY:
> Two, my foot.

JACOB:
> All right, one then. One in particular.

MARY:
> Oh?

JACOB:
> Her name was Rose, and she looked like you. In fact,
> she might've been your spitting image, except for her
> gentle manner.

MARY: *Beat.*
> I'm gentle . . .

JACOB:
> The odd time.

MARY:
> I'm not like this with another soul but you. I've never
> met anyone who makes me cross as a hornet half the time.

JACOB:

Rose was gentle *all* the time. She said I brought out the best in her.

MARY:

There was no Rose. You're making it up. What was her last name?

JACOB:

I'm not much with last names. Rose of Sharon, I called her. 'How beautiful are thy feet with shoes, O prince's daughter!' . . .

MARY: *Beat*

What did you do together, you and this . . . this Rose?

JACOB:

Oh, the odd time we'd go dancing at the Palace Pier. That's a dancehall down by Lake Ontario. Once we took a midnight cruise to Niagara Falls and back. There was a band playing.

MARY:

I don't believe a word of it.

JACOB:

Mostly we'd go to a picture show. My favourite (*last syllable rhymes with 'night'*) was always Tom Mix.

MARY:

Tom Mix? Who in the world is he?

JACOB:

What? You've never heard of the 'King of the Cowboys,' the most famous Western actor alive?

MARY:

No, and I still haven't seen a picture show. I don't have the time or money for such t'ings.

JACOB:

Then I'll take you, maid! Right now!

MARY:

Take me where?

JACOB:

To the pictures, Mary. I'll take you to see Tom Mix in 'The Lucky Horseshoe.' *He sits on the step and pats the area beside him.* Here. Sit down on the step.

MARY: *suspiciously*

What's you up to now?

JACOB: *all innocence*

I'm not up to a blessed t'ing . . .

MARY still regards him with mistrust.

. . . Come on, sit down. I won't bite . . . Will you hurry up, we'll be late for the picture . . .

MARY reluctantly sits down, though she sits at a discreet distance from JACOB.

. . . All right, now it's a Friday night in Toronto, and we'm at the picture house. We just slipped into the last row of the Christie T'eatre on St. Clair. You comfortable?

MARY:

Yes. Only why are we sitting so far back? Why don't we sit in the front?

JACOB:

Why? 'Cause all the front seats are taken, that's why. Jesus, we just sat down, and already you'm complaining.

MARY:

I just wondered why we had to sit in the last row.

JACOB:

I told you, didn't I? These are the only two seats left. Count yourself lucky to get 'em . . . All right, now, the next is important. There are t'ree t'ings, Mary, that a fellow who takes his sweetheart—

MARY:

I'm not your sweetheart.

JACOB:

Suit yourself.

MARY:

Just remember that.

JACOB:

Hush up. The picture's about to begin . . . No, it's just the newsreel . . . Now as I was saying, there are t'ree t'ings that a fellow who takes a girl to the pictures always does in a picture house. And if he don't do all t'ree to his satisfaction, he don't get his fifteen cents worth.

MARY:

What's that?

JACOB:

First off, he lights up a cigarette, if he happens to have a tailor-made. That's number one: a Sweet Caporal.

MARY:

What's number two?

JACOB:

Number two is he cocks his feet on the seat of the fellow ahead, and if the fellow looks back, you stares at him like Tom Mix in 'The Lucky Horseshoe.' A smirky sort of look that makes him slink low in his seat . . . Be quiet now. The picture's just begun . . . Look, there's Tom now, riding up the road on his horse named Tony. That's some wonderful black horse, boy. See how his mane is permed and his tail all combed. And look how smart Tom looks in his same old get-up: silver spurs on the heels of his boots, that leather fit-out over his pants they calls chaps, that hanky knotted around his neck, and that tall hat with the wide brim and the crown stove in on both sides. See how straight Tom sits in the saddle, Mary. You'd swear he had an oar up his arse . . .

MARY:

I don't like language like that, Jacob! So just stop it!

JACOB:

Sorry, maid. It just slipped out.

MARY:

Besides, you said there was t'ree t'ings a fellow did in a picture show. You never mentioned the last.

JACOB:

I was getting to that. Saving the best for later . . . Now there always comes a time in the picture show, Mary, when the fellow you'm with gets the sense . . . the sense that the time is right.

MARY:

The time for what?

JACOB:

Well, say it's me now. I'd glance out of the corner of my eye and see you sitting there with your hair all washed, your hands folded in your lap, looking all soft and lovely and smelling as fresh as the wind, and I'd sort of lean back in my seat like this and slip my arm around you . . .

JACOB does. MARY knocks his arm away and springs to her feet.

MARY: *indignantly*
So this is what you've been doing, is it, in the picture house with Rose?

JACOB:
There is no Rose.

MARY:
I don't believe you!

JACOB:
I made her up.

MARY:
Liar!

JACOB:
Look, will you sit down and watch the picture? This is one of the best Tom ever made. He rides right into a wedding chapel and snatches the bride from under the nose of the groom. *He grins.*

MARY:
I suppose you finds that funny?

JACOB:
It made me stand up, maid, and cheer.

MARY:
That's the most brazen t'ing I ever heard of. Why did he do it in the first place?

JACOB:
Why? 'Cause the girl was being married against her will, why else. Tom rode to the rescue.

MARY:
What if she *wasn't* marrying against her will? What then?

JACOB:

Then there would've been no picture. Besides, she had to be getting married against her will. If you saw the slouch of a bridegroom, you wouldn't have to ask.

MARY:

No odds. He might be full of himself, this . . . this Mr. Tom Mix, but that don't give him the right to barge in and take what's not his.

JACOB:

Go on with you. Sure, even the horse looked pleased. He stood there on the carpet, Tony, all sleek and smug. Tom was sitting in the saddle, clutching the bride on his hip, the train of her gown brushing the floor. All eyes was on Tom. The Maids of Honour in their summer hats all gazed up at him, puzzled, and the minister looked on with his t'umb in the Bible, waiting to see what happened next.

MARY:

What did the groom do? I suppose he just stood by and never lifted a finger?

JACOB:

What could he do, the fool, against the likes of Tom Mix? He raised himself to his full height and gave Tom a dirty look, and Tom gazed right back down at him with that little smirk on his lips, as much as to say, 'Too bad, buddy. Better luck next time.'

Slight pause.

MARY:

Well, Tom Mix had best climb back on his horse and ride off into the night. This is one bride he won't be stealing.

JACOB:
No?

MARY:

No. And he better ride off soon, too, before Mr. and Mrs. Dawe return from the wake.

JACOB:

Nobody puts the run on Tom Mix.

MARY:

Tom Mix is a fool.

JACOB:

No more than you, if you expects me to swallow another one of your lies.

MARY:

What lie's that?

JACOB:

'What lie's that?' she says, knowing full well the Right Honourable and Lady Emma won't be home soon.

MARY:

Indeed they will. They'll be home any minute now.

JACOB:

Indeed they won't. They won't be home till sunrise. Not till Mrs. Foote has had a good night's sleep and can sit vigil at the coffin. I heard 'em say so . . .

MARY says nothing.

. . . So it looks like it's just us, Mary. Just you and me and the moon. You and me and the moon that was meant for Jerome . . .

MARY crosses to the porch and picks up the telescope.

. . . And isn't she a lovely one, too? As white as the wafer in Holy Communion.

MARY: *crossing into the yard*
I'm not speaking to you after this, Jacob. From now on you can talk to yourself, for all the good it'll do . . . *She trains the telescope on the sky, ignoring him.*

JACOB:
That's no way to be, Mary. Rose always liked the way I talked. She said it was . . . oh, what was her word? . . . quaint.

> *MARY doesn't react.*

Sing me a song, Jacob, my son, she'd always say. No one can handle a song like you. *Beat.* Sing me a verse of 'Newfoundland Love Song.' The verse that goes— *He recites very simply.*
'Meet me when all is still
   My Annie fair!
Down by the up-line mill,
   My Annie fair!
Near to the silent grove,
I'll tell you how I love,
While the stars shine above,
   My Annie fair!'

> *MARY turns and regards him with reproach.*

'I can't sing you that one, Rose,' I said. 'That song belongs to a girl back home.'

MARY:
I don't care if you had ten Roses, and you sang all the songs up your sleeve. What odds to me? *She returns to the telescope.*

JACOB:
That's right. What odds to you? You have Jerome McKenzie to comfort you now. And what a comfort he'll be on a winter's night, with his knobby knees and cold feet . . . The wind screeching like a broken heart, and him in the dark, wondering why his wife is

70

turned to the wall, wondering to himself, 'Why is Mary like that? Why is her heart as cold as my feet?' . . .

> *MARY walks to another part of the yard and turns her back on him, lifting the telescope to the sky.*

What do you suppose Jerome's up to right now? Prob'bly sitting on Isaac Tucker's step, whilst Doctor Babcock's inside with Betty. Him and Isaac smoking their pipes, their chins to the sky. 'Look, Isaac, there's King Charles' Wain.' 'King Charles' Wain?' says Isaac. 'Where?' . . .

> *MARY reacts. She lowers the telescope but doesn't look around.*

. . . 'Right there,' says Jerome. 'Right over Spaniard's Bay. See? Some calls it the Plough. Most calls it the Big Dipper. But its real name is Ursa Major. U-r-s-a. Ursa Major. That means the great Bear in a dead language.'

MARY: *turning*
Why, you . . . !

JACOB: *quickly*
Why did you ever agree to it, Mary? Why would you marry someone like that? It don't make sense.

MARY:
Where did you learn so much about the Dipper? Standing there, earlier on, pretending not to know a blessed t'ing!

JACOB:
Sam Boone taught me this winter. He knows the stars like his own hand. Now will you answer my question?

MARY:
What question?

71

JACOB:

You've so much steel inside you, maid. So much fire in your spirit. Why would you waste it on a weak little flame like Jerome? It's not fair to him, and it's not fair to yourself.

MARY: *vehemently*

Fair? What's fair got to do with it? Is it fair that my sister has to live in a Home with an iron fence around it? A fourteen-year-old girl sleeping in a bed with a number on it, her initials inside her shoes in ink? Is that fair?

JACOB:

No, of course not—

MARY:

Well then!

JACOB:

What's that got to do with what I asked?

MARY:

A lot more than you imagines.

JACOB:

Well, there's no need to snap my head off, is there?

MARY:

You any idea how many girls live at the Home? More than a hundred. All between six and sixteen.
Sometimes twenty-one girls to a room. The big girls like Dot get up at five o'clock and make bread. At six she lights the Quebec heater with the galvanized boiler attached. Sometimes it's hard to light, the wood might be wet.

JACOB:

So?

MARY:

So the Matron will come in and put her hand on the boiler. 'This is not hot enough,' she says. 'I couldn't light it, Miss,' says Dot. 'The wood's wet.' And the Matron will knock her to the floor and put her foot on her.

JACOB:

Who told you that?

MARY:

Dot did. Back in June.

JACOB:

Jesus Christ! . . .

MARY:

There's a lot more, but I won't go into it. Dot made me promise not to complain to the Home, the Matron would only make it worse. She can't say a word in her letters, either, or they won't be mailed . . . I went to see her the day we left St. John's this summer. I walked up to Hamilton Avenue and rang the bell. They let me into the siting-room, then Dot came in . . . There was a smudge of stove polish on her cheek. She'd been cleaning the stoves with blackening, and the Matron had struck her. She'd wiped the sting away with her hand, forgetting her fingers was black with polish. I said, 'Dot, go get dressed. I'm taking you out for the day.' And when she came back, she was wearing a pair of laced-up boots, a dark blue hat with elastic under the chin, those navy blue kneesocks turned down, and an old tweed coat with no lining . . . We went back to Mrs. Dawe's and up to my room. I said, 'Take off those clothes, Dot, we're going out.' She looked frightened to death. I said, 'What's wrong?' She said, 'I don't want to take my clothes off.' I said, 'Don't you want to wear this pretty blue dress?' She said, 'I can't take my clothes off, Mary. Don't make me.' 'I won't make you,' I said. 'But why can't you?' And she sat on the bed and looked at her feet . . .

73

'Promise you won't write Mother?' she said. 'Promise you won't tell anyone?' I promised. 'I don't have long to live, Mary,' she said. 'I'm dying.' 'Go on with you,' I said. 'You're fourteen years old. You'll live to be an old woman.' 'No, I won't,' she said. And with that, she lifted up her skirt and showed me her underwear . . .

JACOB:
Her underwear?

MARY: *suddenly embarrassed*
Oh, no odds. It's just that . . .

JACOB:
What?

MARY:
Well, that morning she'd been making her bed as usual. That was when she first noticed it . . .

JACOB:
Noticed what?

MARY:
I can't tell you. Just that she'd become a woman that day and didn't know it. I had to explain it to her, the way Mrs. Dawe explained it to me, and I told her it wasn't a 'curse,' either, which is what Mrs. Dawe called it . . . Then we both had a good laugh, and went out and walked the streets. I pointed out the drugstore where Tommy Ricketts was now the druggist, and we went inside and looked at him. He had the shyest smile and the kindest eyes, and him so brave in the War. The youngest soldier in the British Army to win a Victoria Cross. I almost asked if he remembered Jim Snow, but I was too in awe to speak . . . Once outside, I told Dot who he was, and how she had to be like him. Brave like him and Father, only brave in a different way. I told her the Matron was a coward, and like all cowards, I said, she was cruel, so the next time she puts her foot on you,

74

Dot, I said, don't make a sound: don't even cry out, 'cause she'll only grind her heel into you all the harder. Just look into her eyes, I said, and let her know that no odds how often she knocks you down, no odds how hard she steps on you, the one t'ing she'll never destroy is your spirit. And maybe, just maybe she'd stop doing it, 'cause it's a funny t'ing, I said, about cruel people like the Matron, they only respects one kind of person in the long run, and that's the ones they can't break . . . That night at the station, Mr. Dawe tried to buy me a ticket in Second Class. He always did that. Him and Mrs. Dawe would sit in First Class and he'd buy me a ticket in Second; once we was out of St. John's and the conductor had punched the tickets, he'd come back and say 'All right, Mary, you can come in First Class now.' . . . Only this time I wouldn't let him. I said, 'No, Mr. Dawe, and that you won't! I wants a ticket in First Class and I don't care if I have to pay the extra twenty cents myself!'

JACOB:
Good for you.

MARY:
He bought me the ticket, too, and I sat on the train and looked out the window, vowing I'd get Dot out from behind that iron fence one way or another . . . There's not much more to tell . . . Before too long Jerome was stopping by, all dressed up, with a bag of sweets. Only this time I didn't discourage him. I took the sweets that night, and the oranges the next, and when he showed up one night with a ring in his pocket, I took that, too. That's it.

   Pause.

JACOB:
No, that's not it. That's not it by a long shot. Not as far as I'm concerned.

MARY:

Please, will you just go now? I'd sooner be left alone. I don't want to hear about Tom Mix and his black horse, or girls you went out with called Rose . . .

JACOB:

There was no Rose. You was right the first time. I never took a soul to the picture show and I never went to Niagara Falls.

MARY:

I don't care if you did . . .

JACOB:

Not that I couldn't have, mind. Sam Boone had a niece that used to pester me half to death.

MARY:

Sam Boone has only one niece. Her name is Rachel. She's two years old and lives in Corner Brook.

Slight pause.

JACOB:

Well, it was Sam and Lucy who saw me off at Union Station. That much is true. Before I boarded the train, I said to him, 'Sam,' I said, 'what would you do if you had a girl back home that might still be smitten with you but prob'bly couldn't let on? What advice would you give?' You want to know what he said, Mary?

MARY:

What?

JACOB:

He said, 'Jacob, did you ever hear tell of the Society girl from St. John's who let it be known she'd marry the first Blue Puttee to win a Victoria Cross? Every time they went over the top, the single boys would yell—' *raising his arm in a fist* 'JENNY SAUNDERS OR A WOODEN LEG!'

MARY:
Keep your voice down, for goodness sake! . . .

JACOB:
The best battle cry I ever heard, that.

MARY:
Well, I'm no Society Girl, and you're no Blue Puttee.
So there.

JACOB: *Beat.*
'Besides,' Lucy said, 'if she's still mooning over you,
my son, she'll let you know somehow. It's as simple as
that.'

MARY:
It's not as simple as that, and you knows it. There's
one member of the wedding you forgot to mention,
Jacob, when you told about Tom Mix riding in to steal
the bride. What about him?

JACOB:
Who?

MARY:
Who? The father of the groom, as if you forgot. What
was he doing that day, bent over with laughter? Or
was he standing off to one side, burning up with
shame?

JACOB:
I never noticed.

MARY:
You noticed a lot else.

JACOB:
Is that what you suppose this is, Mary? An eye for an
eye? You t'ink I rode t'ousands of miles by train and
boat, all to get back at Will McKenzie?

MARY:
I'm asking *you* that.

JACOB: *flaring up*
Well, if that's what you really belives, Mary, then
you'm right: I *am* a stranger. More of a stranger than
you realizes. And if that's the sort of man you
imagines me to be, then the hell with you, Mary
Snow! Keep your star-gazing fiancé with his bald spot
and bag of candies! *He slips on his suit jacket and
picks up the suitcase.*

MARY: *pursuing him*
Why shouldn't I wonder that? The same question will
be on everyone else's lips tomorrow.

JACOB:
I don't give a damn what others t'ink! It wouldn't
bother me if the preacher denounced me from the
pulpit! It's what *you* t'inks that matters! You and no
one else! *He starts to exit.*

MARY:
There's no call to carry on like this . . .

JACOB:
Isn't there? You stand there and tell me straight to my
face I'm no better than the Matron—as cruel as her or
Will McKenzie—and you expects me not to raise my
voice?

MARY:
I never meant it the way you took it . . .

JACOB:
Do you really believe I'd ever set out to hurt you?
That I'd use you, just to settle accounts with someone
else?

MARY:

Are you telling me it never crossed your mind? Maybe the night you packed your bag. Maybe the day you walked t'rough Customs at North Sydney. Maybe on the deck of the boat or in your seat on the train to here. Wouldn't it be a slap in the face for Jerome's father to have his son left high and dry at the altar? Be honest!

JACOB:

All right. Yes, it crossed my mind. For as long as a shooting star takes. A flash. A flick of a second. I can't help that, can I? . . . But I never came home the avenging angel, the smell of blood in my nostrils. And if you still don't know why I'm standing here in a store-bought suit, with stockings in my suitcase, then I might as well walk out of this yard, and the sooner the better! All I'm doing is making a fool of myself! *He starts off.*

MARY:

I suppose you expects me to stop you?

JACOB: *stops and turns*

And that I don't. For all I cares, you can sit in that rocker and polish your ring . . . I won't be troubling you again, Mary. So goodnight to you. *He starts off again.*

MARY: *pursuing him*

Not goodnight, Jacob! Goodbye!

JACOB:

Suit yourself. Goodbye then. At least now you won't have to slap my face.

> *He exits down the road stage left, leaving behind a sudden, terrible silence. MARY takes a step or two after him, then begins to quickly chant the words of the song we first heard JACOB singing. The tone is defiant, as though she were thumbing her nose at him.*

MARY:

Oh, the moon shines bright on Charlie Chaplin,
His boots are crackin' for the want of blackin'
And his baggy trousers they want mending . . .

*And suddenly the words choke in her throat and she sobs
into her hands all the feelings she has stored inside her for
the past year. Her hands try to stifle the sobs as if her
soul were rushing from her mouth and she was trying to
push it back inside . . . It is a sudden short-lived burst
of emotion. She raises her head and looks down the road.
She takes another step or two.*

MARY: *tentatively*

Jacob . . .   *louder*   Jacob! . . .   *Then she lets
out a cry that splits apart the night.*   JAAACOOOB!

*MARY stands looking down the road, her eyes straining to
see, her eyes almost listening . . . but there is only the empty
road, the moonlight, the silence . . . She composes herself
and returns to the porch step. She sits gazing at some middle
distance, absently turning her engagement ring on her finger.*

*At that moment JACOB walks quietly back onto the road,
still carrying his suitcase, his fedora cocked at a jaunty
angle. There is no grin on his face, however, as he stands
staring at MARY for a long moment, waiting for her to
notice him . . . Finally, she does. She rises, but remains
standing on the porch, looking at him.*

JACOB:

You had me worried there. I t'ought for a minute you
wasn't going to call.   *Now he grins.*

MARY:

Oh, you . . . !

*She raises her elbow and clenches her fist in a parody of a
threatening gesture. A gesture that is not coy but more the
gesture of exasperation a woman might feel who is taken
for granted.*

JACOB:
Now she makes a fist. Took you long enough,
maid . . .

MARY turns away.

. . . And such a little fist, too. Wouldn't bruise a
humming-bird, let alone the King of the
Cowboys . . .

MARY: *still turned away*
So sure of yourself, aren't you, Tom? A real lady-
killer, that's you.

JACOB:
Tom has a modest nature, Mary. He don't like to
boast. Not like some I could name. *He walks a few*
feet closer. Sets the suitcase down in the yard and stands beside it.
On a night like this he'd sooner howl at the moon.
One last shout of joy for old Bob Foote. *He lifts his*
face to the sky and cups his hands around his mouth.

MARY:
Don't you dare! You've already woke up half of
Conception Bay as it is . . .

JACOB drops his hands to his sides, but remains gazing
at the sky. Pause.

JACOB:
God, you can't beat the mystery of it, can you? It's
some wonderful sight. With or without a spyglass.

MARY:
Yes. *She sits and looks up at the heavens.* There are
stars up there that Father was watching the night
before Beaumont Hamel. The light those stars gave off
that night is just reaching us now.

JACOB:
Imagine.

MARY:

There are other stars whose light won't reach here till long after we're gone. Hundreds of years or more. T'ousands.

JACOB:

Jesus, don't get morbid on me. Old Bob wouldn't want that, would he? *He glances at MARY. She returns his glance.*

Slight pause.

MARY:

Was there really a Rose?

JACOB:

Yes.

MARY:

There was not.

JACOB:

All right, there wasn't.

Slight pause.

MARY:

There was, wasn't there?

JACOB:

No. *Beat.* Besides, the past is best forgotten, someone once said. Leave it buried . . .

MARY looks away in mild exasperation.

. . . It's the future that counts, Mary. And the future is here. It's here in this yard right now. It's you and me and that battered old suitcase.

MARY:

Yes, held together with a piece of rope. Some future.

JACOB kneels down in the yard and unties the rope on the suitcase. He looks over at MARY.

JACOB:
Don't be fooled by appearances, Mary. I've got more than songs up my sleeve. I've got your future and mine, all neatly folded on top of my plaid shirts and diamond socks. *He lifts the top of the suitcase and removes a pair of silk stockings, draping them over his arm.* All you have to do, Mary, is reach out, and old Bob can rest tonight with a grin on his face. *then* Well?

MARY: *Beat.*
What about my sister? Are you forgetting her?

JACOB:
I'm not forgetting.

MARY rises from the step. She crosses slowly into the road, but remains well away from JACOB. She stands looking out front as though her eyes are on a distant star. Finally, she speaks.

MARY: *evenly, with great seriousness*
In the years to come, Jacob Mercer—and this is no idle t'reat, mind—in the years to come, if you ever mentions Rose of Sharon, even in your sleep, I'll make you regret the night you knelt in this yard with those stockings in your hand and the moon for a witness. Do you understand me? *She turns and stares at JACOB.* Do you?

JACOB smiles up at the serious face of this lovely young girl. His smile becomes a grin, until it is splitting his face from ear to ear.

Blackout.